THE CELEBRITY CAT CAPER

created by

GERTRUDE CHANDLER WARNER

Illustrated by Anthony VanArsdale

Albert Whitman & Company
Chicago, Illinois

Library of Congress Cataloging-in-Publication
data is on file with the publisher.

ISBN 978-0-8075-0711-7 (hardcover)
ISBN 978-0-8075-0712-4 (paperback)

Printed in the United States of America
10 9 8 7 6 5 4 3 2 1 LB 20 19 18 17 16

Illustrated by Anthony VanArsdale

For more information about Albert Whitman & Company,
visit our web site at www.albertwhitman.com.

Contents

THE CELEBRITY CAT CAPER

CHAPTER 1

Walter the Cog

"It's Sunday!" Six-year-old Benny Alden bounded into the boxcar where his brother and two sisters were waiting. A few kernels of popcorn fell out of the large bowl he carried and landed on the floor. "Oops," Benny said. Balancing the bowl in one hand, he bent to clean up the mess, but Watch, the family's wire-haired terrier, got there first. He gobbled up the popcorn then looked up at Benny expectantly.

"No people snacks for you," Benny told

Watch. "It's Sunday! Popcorn is the second-best part of Sunday nights."

"What's the first best part?" asked Violet as she gave Watch a dog treat. Her brown pigtails bounced as she held back a laugh. She was just teasing Benny. She knew watching funny videos was her little brother's favorite part of Sunday night.

The four Alden children were very close. When their parents died, they had been on their own. They had found an old boxcar in the woods and made it their home instead of living with Grandfather Alden. They had heard he was mean. But when Grandfather finally found them, the children quickly realized they'd been wrong—he wasn't mean at all. Now the children lived with him in Greenfield and their boxcar was in the backyard for a clubhouse.

Benny grabbed a big handful of popcorn before passing it to his fourteen-year-old brother, Henry, but lost a few more kernels. "Oops," Benny said again as Watch ate the fallen kernels and lay down at their feet, waiting for anything else that dropped.

Jessie opened up her laptop. At twelve years old, she had a knack for finding interesting and useful information on the Internet. It was Jessie who'd first discovered the Walter the Cat videos and shown the others.

Benny took another handful of popcorn, "I can't wait to find out what the *cog* was up to this week!"

"Cog?" Violet asked. "Did you make up a new word?"

Benny just grinned.

"I get it," said Henry. "*Cat* plus *dog* equals *cog*!" He reached over to ruffle Benny's short dark brown hair. "And Walter is a cat who acts like a dog. That's very clever," he said.

"I know!" Benny said, "But…I didn't make it up." He unzipped his sweatshirt jacket to reveal a new T-shirt underneath. It was bright blue with a big picture of Walter, a sleek brown and beige Bengal cat. Under the picture was a single word in gold letters: "COG."

"It's from the mall," Benny said. "I picked it out and bought it with my birthday gift card." He puffed out his chest so the others could see.

"Walter is a cog!" Benny laughed. Soon he was laughing so hard he nearly fell into the popcorn bowl. Henry playfully pushed him into a beanbag chair instead. Benny flopped over and continued to laugh, holding his belly. "Cog, cog, cog..."

Henry shook his head. "Come on! Save some laughs for Walter." He dragged the beanbag with Benny still on it over to where his brother could see the screen. Violet pulled another beanbag over and made room for both Henry and herself.

Jessie typed in the web address for Walter the Cat's page and looked through the list of videos. "Here's a funny one," she said. "But we've seen it before."

"It doesn't matter," Benny said. "We'll see a new one next. Play it, Jessie! Pleeease..."

Jessie clicked on the video so that it filled the screen.

The video began with Walter the Cat walking across an expensive-looking rug in a large living room. He appeared very royal with his gleaming coat. On his forehead, between his eyes, the coloring in his fur formed a *W*.

A woman's voice came from offscreen. "Bang! Bang!" she called.

Walter dropped to the ground and played dead.

The woman commanded, "Roll over." And Walter rolled over and over.

"Up," said the voice, and Walter stood on his back legs and walked like a circus dog.

"Good, Walter," the voice said. Then the video ended.

"That's one of my favorites!" Benny said. "Play another, Jessie. A new one."

Jessie was scrolling though the list of videos. "I don't understand what's going on here," she said. "We've seen these all before."

"Mrs. Beresford always posts new videos on Sundays," Henry said.

The children had seen many Walter the Cat videos. They knew the videos were always posted by Walter's owner, Mrs. Beresford, even though she never appeared in them.

"Some of those other cat videos have their owners in them, but she's a mysterious woman," Benny said. "That makes me like her even more!"

"Nothing like a good mystery," Violet agreed with a chuckle.

"Hmmm..." Jessie muttered to herself as she stared at the screen. "Walter's new videos usually make Pick of the Week on this website, but he's not on the list this time. That's odd. There must be a new video in here somewhere."

"Could you play an old one while you're looking?" Benny asked.

Jessie opened another window. "Here's the latest one. But it's from two weeks ago. There wasn't a new video last weekend either."

She searched the list while her siblings watched the two-week-old video in the other window.

In this video, Walter panted like a dog and made a barking sound. It must have sounded like a real bark to Watch, who stood up and stared at the screen with his tail wagging.

"Fantastic!" Benny clapped when it was over. "Will you play the one where Walter shakes paws?"

Jessie loaded the video with a sigh. "Why can't I find anything new?"

Henry offered to look over the list. He took Jessie's spot at the computer while Violet and Benny watched the shaking-paws video.

"Strange," Henry said, pushing his brown hair off his face. "Mrs. Beresford has posted a Walter video every Sunday—until last week. She's been doing it for almost a year."

Jessie reached over to the keyboard and typed "Walter the Cog" into a new search window. "I wonder why she stopped."

"Maybe she's on vacation," Violet offered.

"Hey, look!" Jessie said. "I found something."

Violet and Benny leaned closer to the screen. Jessie had opened up a new browser window to a page called Cog Chat. It was a message board for people who wanted to talk about Walter the Cat.

"Now that we know that Walter's nickname is 'Cog' we can find more stuff about him online," Jessie said. "Look at this..."

She pointed to a message posted by someone called "WalterTruthTeller."

Henry read it aloud. *"Walter does not perform his own tricks. The videos are all fake."*

"No way!" Benny said.

Jessie found several more online discussions about Walter the Cat. WalterTruthTeller had posted the same message in each one. "The name is everywhere with accusations all over the place, but I can't figure out who it is."

"How could anyone say Walter isn't doing his own tricks?" Violet asked. "It's right there in the videos."

Henry read some of the posts over Jessie's shoulder. "WalterTruthTeller says that the videos are manipulated with film software," Henry explained. "Like Hollywood movie-making."

Benny moved closer to the screen. "WalterTruthTeller is wrong."

"So many strange things are going on," Jessie said as she read. "No new videos for two weeks and now these terrible comments meant to ruin Walter's reputation." She looked at some of the newest messages. "This one says that Walter should go back to the animal shelter where he came from!"

"What do you think it all means?" Violet asked.

"Sounds like the beginning of a mystery," Henry said.

"I think we should investigate," Jessie said. "But where do we begin?"

"I don't know," Henry said. "Anyone have an idea?"

Just then the boxcar door opened.

"Benny..." Grandfather stepped inside. "This came for you in the mail today." He handed Benny an envelope. "Remember how we signed up for the Cog Fan Club when you bought your T-shirt? This looks like the welcome letter."

"It has my address on it!" Benny waved the envelope around. "I got mail!" He opened the letter and handed it to Grandfather. "Can you help me read it, please?"

Grandfather pushed his reading glasses up on his nose and scanned the text. "Well, now, there's a surprise."

"What?" Henry and Benny asked at the same time.

"This is a list of fun facts about Walter. He's four years old, chases mice, and"—he paused dramatically—"Mrs. Beresford lives here in Greenfield."

"Really?" Violet asked.

"In an old mansion at the edge of town." He rubbed his chin. "I know the house. I just never knew who lived there."

"Walter lives in Greenfield!" Benny said, clasping his hands to his heart. "This is the happiest day in my whole life!"

"And now we know where to begin our investigation," Henry said.

CHAPTER 2

The Beresford Will

Benny was awake before the others the next day. Henry found him sitting in the kitchen eating cereal and reading something on their tablet.

"It's the Cog Newsletter," Benny said, between bites of crispy corn flakes. "But it's from two weeks ago." He sighed.

"Maybe we'll learn something new about Walter today," Henry told him. The children planned to ride their bikes by the Beresford mansion to see if they could spot any sign of the cat. "Maybe he'll be sitting in the window and we'll know everything is fine."

"Can we go now?" Benny asked his brother. "I woke up with a weird feeling in my belly. I thought it was hunger, but now I think it's worry." He pushed his bowl aside. "We should wake up everyone and go over there as fast as we can. I'll go get my bike out of the garage."

"Aren't you going to wait for us?" Jessie said as she and Violet entered the kitchen. Jessie was holding a notebook and pen.

Violet wasn't quite as prepared for the day out. Her hair, usually tied back in pigtails, was long and messy. She yawned. "Jessie woke me up."

"I couldn't sleep," Jessie said. "I can't stop thinking about who would post such mean things about Walter on the Internet, and why." She held up her notebook. "We are going to find out!"

"Can we go now?" Benny asked. His hand was on the knob to the back door.

"It's too early," Henry said, checking the clock. "It's Saturday morning, and only seven o'clock!"

Benny's shoulders sank. "I bet Walter is up though. He's a busy cat." He glanced at Watch, who was sleeping under the kitchen table. "Unlike this sleepyhead."

"Watch isn't a sleepyhead." Jessie laughed, then corrected herself. "He's awake sometimes." At that, Watch raised his head, yawned, then went right back to sleep. Jessie said, "Let the rest of us get breakfast, then we'll go."

Watch let out a big snore.

"I suppose I could eat breakfast again," Benny said. He sat back down in his chair and poured himself another bowl of cereal.

***

The bike ride to the Beresford mansion seemed short compared to the ride up the big house's driveway. The children went through the ornately carved open gates and rode for what seemed like forever to get to the enormous house at the top of the hill.

Benny huffed as his short legs struggled to move the bike uphill. Henry asked if he wanted to take a break, but Benny was determined. "Walter needs us," he said between big gulps of air.

It wasn't Benny who was the slowest. Violet was having trouble with her bike chain. It kept skipping and made a strange rattling noise. She pulled to the side. "Hang on. I'll be right there," she called to the others.

Jessie nodded in reply as she, Henry, and Benny rode around a bend in the driveway. "We'll wait over here," she called to Violet.

Violet was fiddling with the chain when a noise behind her made her turn. A black limousine was moving slowly up the driveway toward the house. She moved over onto the grass to let the limo pass, but instead it slowed and stopped beside her. The back window rolled down and a young woman peered out. She was in a black dress and hat with a matching dark veil. "Are you here for the reading of the will?" she asked.

Violet, still sweaty from the bike ride, glanced down at her T-shirt and jeans. It seemed pretty obvious to her that she wasn't headed to anything that required nice clothes. "The will?" Violet repeated, confused.

The woman raised her veil. She was very pale and Violet wondered if she'd ever been

in the sun. She had light skin, light hair, and
narrow eyebrows. Violet guessed she was
about college age. "My aunt's will, of course,"
the woman said. "Mrs. Beresford. She passed
away two weeks ago."

"You mean…died?" Violet whispered. "Oh,
I'm so sorry."

The young woman nodded. "She simply died
of old age. The doctor said her time had come.
She lived a long and happy life, you know."

Violet felt a little better hearing that. And
now she knew why there hadn't been new
Walter videos. But now she wondered about
Walter. Who was taking care of him?

The young woman interrupted Violet's
thoughts. "Well, if you aren't here for the
reading of the will, why are you here? There's
only one house at the end of this driveway."

Violet didn't know what to say. "We…we
came about Walter," she stammered.

"That's good news. That cat must leave the
house," the woman said. "I assume you'll be
taking him away with you today then."

"We aren't planning to—" Violet started
when Henry interrupted.

"Violet!" He was biking back toward her. "Do you need help? The others are waiting to—" Henry stopped pedaling and stared at the limousine.

Violet quickly explained that today was the reading of Mrs. Beresford's will. "This is her niece," she told her brother.

"Natalie," the woman said to them both. "Natalie Beresford. I'm the daughter of Beulah Beresford's brother."

Henry nodded and said politely, "Nice to meet you."

"Well," Natalie said, suddenly becoming impatient. "Come along then. If you are here to take the cat, I definitely won't stop you. I'll gladly help pack his stuff up! Leave the bikes and I'll have Geoffrey return to collect them." She opened the limo door to the children. "Get in."

Henry and Violet exchanged confused glances.

"Thank you, but we'll ride our bikes," Henry said. "Our brother and sister are just ahead."

"Suit yourself," Natalie said, closing the

car door with a bang. "But you'd better hurry. The reading of the will begins in fifteen minutes." The limo sped off, leaving Violet and Henry by the side of the road.

"She's odd," Henry said, as they watched the limousine disappear. "And she seems to hate that cat."

"Do you think she's WalterTruthTeller?" Violet asked with a frown. "Not that it matters anymore. This mystery is solved. Mrs. Beresford died, so that's why there are no new videos, right?"

"I guess so," Henry said. He got off his bike to walk with Violet. "And WalterTruthTeller might be trying to make Walter look bad, but if there won't be new videos, there's no point anymore. And no use trying to find out who he is." He sighed. "Benny is going to be so upset that there aren't new Walter videos. What will we do on Sunday nights?"

They met Benny and Jessie at a cement bench beneath a large shade tree not far from the house. Henry told them the news about Mrs. Beresford and about meeting Natalie.

Benny's eyes widened. "Oh no!"

"I'm sure Walter will be all right," Jessie sighed. "But we shouldn't be here."

Violet agreed. "We should go home," she said. "The reading of the will is for family."

They were about to start walking home with their bikes when a figure appeared in front of them on the driveway. It was the driver of the limousine, an older man wearing a chauffeur's cap and a black suit with a narrow bow tie.

"I believe we've met before," he said. "Your grandfather is James Alden, yes? I'm Geoffrey Bigg."

"Oh…hello," Henry said, shaking the man's hand. He knew Mr. Bigg was a school friend of Grandfather's, because he had come to a party at their house. Jessie recognized him too. Sometimes it seemed like everyone in town knew Grandfather.

"I'm glad you're here, and I hear you have come for Walter," Geoffrey said, giving the children a look of great concern.

"Well," Jessie tried to explain. "We were just riding by to see if he was all right, but—"

"Then you must hurry," Geoffrey said. "Walter is in trouble. You must save him!"

Henry and Violet looked at Benny and Jessie.

"Walter needs us!" Benny said. He pointed to the mansion, which was just ahead. "Call Grandfather, Henry. Ask if we can go inside."

Henry called Grandfather and then handed the phone to Geoffrey. Grandfather agreed to let the children visit the mansion for a few minutes to meet Walter. Then he would come to pick them up since Violet's bicycle wasn't working. Soon Geoffrey was leading them to the front steps of the mansion, which sat behind a tree-lined circular driveway.

"Go!" he said. "The reading of the will is about to begin. You must be there from the start."

"But," Violet said. "We aren't related to Mrs. Beresford..."

"I know..." Geoffrey said with a curt nod. "But if not you...who will help that poor cat?" He got into the limousine and sped away.

"Things are getting stranger and stranger," Henry said, watching the car disappear around the back of the house.

"Whoa." Benny looked up at the huge

mansion. He gasped when he tried to count the windows on the front of the house. There were a lot, maybe more than one hundred!

"Come on," Henry said, and they rushed up the stone stairway to the enormous double doors. The doorway was surrounded by large statues of cats. And not just any cat—it was clear that Walter had been the model for each statue. Two stone-carved Walters sat regally to either side of the doors; above, another stone Walter lay on his back in roll-over motion. Each door had brass cat door knockers above brass cat doorknobs, which were carvings of Walter.

Violet was an artist herself. "I wonder if there are paintings too," she said aloud. "I'm not really into sculpture, but I'd love to see oils or charcoals or even watercolors of Walter."

"Maybe there are some inside?" Henry suggested.

The doors to the house were open slightly, so the children let themselves in.

There were more Walter statues scattered around the front foyer. But instead of stone, these were bronze and sat on marble podiums:

Walter on his hind legs. Walter in a cat bed, napping. Walter on the prowl.

"What's he doing in this one?" Jessie asked, leaning in toward the statue closest to her. It showed Walter carrying a piece of paper in his mouth, his legs crouched as if running.

"He's chasing the mailman," Benny said. "He's a cog, remember?"

"Of course," Jessie said, shaking her head and stepping back.

The sound of voices at the end of a long hallway drew their attention.

"Must be the reading of the will," Jessie said, leading the way.

"This is awkward," Violet said, trying to smooth her T-shirt. "We aren't dressed very neatly and we didn't even know Mrs. Beresford."

"But Geoffrey said Walter needs us," Benny reminded her.

"But we aren't family," she countered. As Violet tried to convince the others they should leave, Natalie Beresford came out of a side room with a man who looked about the same age she was. They were talking softly.

"If we knock out this wall, we will have plenty of room for the stage," Natalie told the man.

"Things are about to change," Matt said. "It's time for that chauffeur to retire."

Violet realized they meant Geoffrey.

"There will be no need to keep the cat nanny on staff another second either," Natalie quickly added. "I've never liked that girl."

"She's our cousin," Matt said with a laugh. "And not much younger than us!"

Natalie snorted. "That doesn't mean I have to like her. When we own the house, Olivia will be the first to go." Natalie turned and looked down the hallway. "These are the children I told you about," Natalie said, raising her voice and pointing at Violet and the others. "They've come for Walter."

"Fantastic!" he cheered. "I'm Matt Beresford, Natalie's brother. We are thrilled to hear the cat will be taken care of." He reached out and shook Henry's hand. "With Walter safely away, Natalie and I will move our business here." He pointed out a large window near where they stood. "There's another house on the property. It's been rented for years to an eccentric sculptor. Obviously, this is his work." He waved his hand toward the bronze statues in the hall. "The man has a dog, but I plan to move in there once the will is settled. They'll need to leave."

"I'll take the main house," Natalie said. She winked at her brother and smiled. "It's all arranged."

Continuing their plans, they walked together toward a room nearby. The children hung back in the hall.

"They're kind of mean," Jessie whispered to Violet.

"They really want to get rid of Walter," Violet whispered back.

Benny squished in between his sisters. He was feeling anxious. "Maybe we should find Walter," he began, when an older woman came into the hallway. She wore a gray and brown plaid business suit. Her hair was swept into a gray colored bun at the nape of her neck—not one hair out of place.

"I am Mrs. Hudson, the lawyer," she

announced. "We must begin." Natalie and Matt came back out into the hallway.

"We really shouldn't be—" Violet began to protest, but Matt interrupted her, speaking up as if the children weren't even there.

"Will this take long, Mrs. Hudson?" Matt said impatiently.

"Not at all," Mrs. Hudson said. "I need only to inform you and Natalie that you will never move into this house. The house, everything in it, and all of Mrs. Beresford's millions of dollars has been left…to her cat, Walter."

CHAPTER 3

The Late Mrs. Beresford

"Everything?" Natalie replied. Her voice was low and very clearly angry. "Every penny?"

"All of it," Mrs. Hudson said, flipping through the pages of the will to show Natalie and Matt their aunt's signature. "That means every lightbulb and doorknob, plus all the money Mrs. Beresford made when she was selling real estate."

As Mrs. Hudson explained, Mrs. Beresford had come to Greenfield as a young woman with no money. She started out as a gardener at the house, when it belonged to another family. She moved up from cook to maid and when the owners decided to retire to Florida, they left the house to her. That was fifty years ago. In the early days, Mrs. Beresford used the house as an office to sell real estate and built up a very busy business, investing wisely and earning millions of dollars before she died.

"How many millions are we talking?" A voice came from the back of the room.

Violet and Jessie quickly turned around. There was a young woman they hadn't seen before. She was in her early twenties, blond, with her hair curled over her shoulders and was wearing casual jeans and a T-shirt. The Aldens wondered when she'd arrived. And they couldn't help but notice the cat she was carrying.

"Look...there's Walter!" Benny whispered loudly. Natalie turned to him with a fiery look in her eyes.

"Of course she's carrying Walter," Natalie hissed. "Olivia Robie is the babysitter."

"I *prefer* to be called the cat nanny,"

Olivia said, as she crossed the room toward them. "My work is more important than just babysitting. I take care of all of Walter's needs." She turned to Mrs. Hudson. "Now," she asked, "exactly how many millions are we talking about?"

Olivia turned Walter in her arms so he was facing the children. She stroked his head and he purred like a normal cat, not an extraordinary video star.

"Fifty million," the lawyer said.

Natalie gasped. Matt's face turned red.

"Wow!" Benny whispered. "That'll buy a lot of tuna!"

"And that amount doesn't include the house, jewelry, cars, or Walter's sailboat in Florida," the lawyer added. "Those are worth many more millions." She quickly added, "Of course, none of those things can be sold. They all belong to Walter and he must be allowed to vacation or go for a drive whenever he wants."

Henry leaned over to Jessie. "Mrs. Hudson isn't acting like this is strange at all, is she? I mean, leaving a fortune to a cat? And letting him decide when he wants to go out for a ride in the car?"

"It's definitely odd," Jessie agreed.

"Not to me. I am no ordinary lawyer," Mrs. Hudson said, overhearing. "I specialize in pets." She shot a stern look at Natalie and Matt. "Let me assure you, the will is solid. No court will counter it." She grinned. "I'm the best lawyer in Greenfield. That's why your aunt hired me." She turned to the young woman and added, "Olivia, you will remain on staff, well paid to care for Walter. And Geoffrey Bigg cannot be fired. Ever."

"Wow!" Benny exclaimed.

"Mrs. Beresford loved Walter very much," Mrs. Hudson said. "She wanted him to have the best."

Natalie raised her hand to ask a question. "What happens when Walter dies?"

Benny reached out and squeezed Henry's hand. "She's not going to kill him, is she?" he whispered.

Mrs. Hudson heard Benny's question and said, "In the event of Walter's death, all the money will be given to the animal shelter where she first adopted her cat." She turned the will's pages to Natalie and Matt so they could see the signature.

"I see that Geoffrey Bigg is not at this meeting." Mrs. Hudson turned to Matt. "I assume you told him he wasn't needed, since you thought he would be fired this afternoon."

He frowned. "I might have suggested he start packing."

She nodded. "I must go find him then and tell him to unpack." And with that Mrs. Hudson swept from the room.

Just a moment later Natalie turned on Olivia. "You're behind this! I know you are!" She shouted. *"You hate that cat!"*

Olivia put a hand over Walter's ears. "You're scaring the kitty," she said. "Stop yelling, cousin."

"Don't call me 'cousin,'" Natalie screamed. "You're related by marriage, not blood! I know you influenced the will. You came here without any money and now," she pointed at Walter, "thanks to that cat, you live in a mansion and are being paid more money than you could dream of. All you have to do is babysit!"

"Cat *nanny*," Olivia corrected. "I am much more than a babysitter! And in case you've forgotten, I went to college! I have talents that you only wish you had!" As her voice got louder and louder, Walter started squirming in her hands so she set him down. He took off down the hall. "Look what you've done!" Olivia raised her voice. "You scared him away."

"I hope he ran away forever!" Matt broke in. "You don't deserve that cat. I know what a liar and cheat you are!"

"I am not!" Olivia countered.

The fight got louder, with more shouting and a lot of name-calling. When Natalie threw a glass plate across the room, Benny covered his ears and shivered.

"I think we should go," Henry told the others. "And fast!" He led them back into the hallway.

"Can we find Walter first?" Benny begged. "He really did seem scared by all the shouting. I was scared too!"

"Sure. We can check on Walter first," Jessie said. "Plus I want to explore something that's bothering me." They all turned to face her. "Why did Geoffrey insist we go to the reading of the will? He knew we didn't belong here, and yet he said that Walter needed our help."

"He was really insistent. We should find out why," Violet said.

"Walter went this way." Benny led them down the main hallway and into a large patio room with huge glass windows that overlooked the grassy yard behind the house. At the back of the yard was the guesthouse. Jessie remembered hearing that the sculptor lived there.

As the children looked out, they saw a flash of gray fur near the fence around the guesthouse's backyard. "There he is!" Benny said. He pointed out Walter, settling down on top of a fence rail.

"How'd he get out of the house?" Jessie asked, looking around. The doors were all closed.

"Cog door," a man's voice said from behind them. Geoffrey Bigg was standing in the room.

Benny looked down and found there was a small pet door at their feet. "Cog door," he echoed Mr. Biggs. "That's funny."

"Mrs. Beresford had a wonderful sense of humor," Geoffrey said. "We are going to miss her very much." The moment of quiet in the patio room was suddenly filled with shouts from down the hallway. He sighed. "Some of us will miss her more than others," he added.

"Why did you tell us Walter was in trouble?" Jessie asked.

"He is," Geoffrey said. "Too many people are trying to find a way around the will. And they are all determined to get Mrs. Beresford's money. Plus, have you heard about WalterTruthTeller?" The Aldens all nodded and Geoffrey shook his head. "Something is not right. I feel it in my bones."

Henry wanted to ask him more about WalterTruthTeller, but just then there was another loud shout from the other room.

"We just want the house!" Matt shouted.

And Olivia replied, "You don't need the house!"

"Easy for you to say," Natalie shouted, her

voice echoing. "You get to stay in the house, ride in a limo, and go on Walter's boat any time you want—all thanks to that ridiculous cat!"

"You're so dramatic!" Olivia countered. "This isn't a play. It's real life!"

Their voices faded as they went into a farther room.

Geoffrey shook his head. He muttered, "Someday I am going to retire and buy myself an island where none of these greedy Beresford cousins can find me!" He opened the back door to the yard and pointed out at Walter. "But until then, I'll go back to my job and it's time for you to go to work as well. I've heard from your grandfather that you help lots of people. Now you can help Walter."

With that, he left the room. The children looked at one another.

"What should we do?" Violet asked.

"Well, we have a little more time before Grandfather picks us up," Jessie said. "We might as well stick around." She took out her notebook. "If there is any real chance that Walter is in danger, we better find out what's going on."

Chapter 4

Cog Training

The children went out to explore the backyard of the mansion.

"I think we could fit ten boxcars in this yard," Benny said, looking at the green grassy area. He thought about it, then changed his mind, "Eleven."

Henry laughed.

Walter was still sitting on the fence in front of the guesthouse as the children approached. He didn't leap off or even move, and as the children got closer they could see that he was watching something in the side yard of the guesthouse.

"Look, there's a dog here," Jessie said.

In the yard of the guesthouse was an obstacle course for dogs, and a yellow and tan Labrador retriever was going through it while a young man called out commands.

The obstacle course began with a hoop for the dog to jump through. Then the dog zigzagged around cones and walked across a narrow log that lay across a kiddie pool filled with water. When the dog finished, the man gave him a treat and said, "Way to go, Pepper. Good boy."

"Do you think Watch could do that?" Benny asked Jessie. Watch was really Jessie's dog since she'd found him. She had a passion for animals and knew a lot about them.

"I'm not sure," Jessie said. "But it would be fun to try!"

The man came over to the fence. "Hello," he greeted the children. "Were you at the house for the reading of the will?"

"Sort of," Henry answered truthfully. "We were dragged in without really understanding what was going on."

"Interesting." The man nodded. "I could hear the yelling from here. They always fight like cats and dogs when they are together. I take it Natalie and Matt didn't get what they wanted?"

"No," Jessie said. "Mrs. Beresford left everything to Walter."

"That's what I expected," the man said with a smile, then paused for a moment. "I'm guessing they won't let sleeping dogs lie."

"What does that mean?" Benny asked.

Jessie answered, "That means they aren't going to give up and let Walter have all the money."

"Those two are up to something," the man said. "They've been planning something for a long time, and they aren't going to roll over and play dead."

Maybe that's what Mr. Bigg was warning us about, Jessie thought.

"Are you the artist who lives here?" Henry asked the man.

"Sculptor, painter, handyman, dog trainer...you name it, I'll try it. I'm Robert

Morales. Call me Robbie." He tossed back his light brown hair.

"You have a lot of jobs around here," Jessie remarked.

Robbie shrugged. "I always did what Mrs. B. asked. I never bite the hand that feeds me." His green eyes sparkled. "Want to see something amazing?"

"Yes, please!" Violet said. "I really hope it's more of your art. I like your sculptures." Violet was most interested in Robbie's artist jobs. "I draw and paint. Do you have any paintings of Walter?"

"Sure. I'll show you another time," he said, waving dismissively. "But honestly, I'm not all that good. And my easel is broken… it's missing part of the chain that holds it up. So I haven't painted in a while. I prefer sculpture." He paused and frowned. "But no one ever bought my art except Mrs. B. Now that she's gone, I don't know what I'll do… or where I'll live." Shaking off the problem, he called Pepper. "Come." The dog sauntered over and sat at his feet. "You saw what Pepper did in the obstacle course, right?"

The children nodded.

"Now check this out." Robbie called Walter using the same tone of voice he used for Pepper. "Come." The cat jumped off the fence and also went to sit by Robbie's feet. Robbie then pointed at the obstacle course. "Go," he commanded.

Walter started in right away, doing the exact same route that Pepper had just finished. He went through the hoop, around the cones, and walked carefully across the log. When he was done, he came back to Robbie and lay down next to Pepper.

"I don't even have to train that cat," Robbie said. "He's incredible. I show him something once, and he does it! That's all it takes." He smiled. "Walter can do anything. Absolutely anything!"

"That is amazing," Violet agreed. Benny applauded.

"I couldn't believe it myself when it first happened," Robbie said. "It was about a year ago. I didn't even notice that sly cat sitting quietly on the fence. When I finished with Pepper, Walter simply jumped down into the

yard and did everything I'd been working on just like the dog. And to my surprise, without any mistakes!"

"How long had Walter been watching? Was he alone?" Henry asked, glancing back toward the house. "I thought Olivia was always supposed to be with him."

"Olivia, the babysitter?" Robbie snorted.

"Cat nanny," Violet corrected.

The Aldens realized just then that Olivia hadn't come looking for Walter yet. But wasn't that her job?

"Sure...cat nanny," Robbie repeated. "She's worthless. If she wasn't family, she'd have gone back to wherever she came from a long, long time ago. It was one of those days when she'd lost track of Walter again...and of course, like a million times before, Olivia was nowhere to be found. Mrs. B. came looking herself. She loved that cat like a dog loves a bone. That was when Mrs. B. saw Walter copy all of Pepper's tricks."

"Was she surprised?" asked Jessie.

"She said she didn't realize you could teach an old dog new tricks." He laughed. "I told her that Walter was an old cat, so it didn't apply!" Robbie chuckled again, holding his belly. "No one knows how old that cat is, but he sure can learn tricks!"

"That's for sure," Violet said.

Robbie went on. "Mrs. B. asked what else he could do. I didn't know. So we tested him. Turned out that fancy feline had learned everything I'd ever shown Pepper."

Robbie went to a hose and filled two water bowls. One for Walter and one for Pepper and set them side-by-side. "Mrs. B. wanted to make videos. I helped. And the rest is Internet history."

Jessie turned to a clean page in her notebook. "Can I ask you some questions?" she asked Robbie. "We've been warned that something bad might happen to Walter. Do you have any idea why someone might hurt him?"

"I can't imagine anyone hurting Walter. He's the best cat ever. But, I guess if I was *forced* to say why someone would hurt him...well, someone might want the mansion," Robbie suggested, adding quickly, "and the millions."

Henry asked, "Did you know there is a Cog Fan Club?"

"Nope," Robbie said. "But then again, I suppose every dog has his day."

Violet told Benny, "That means anyone, or thing, can be famous for a little while."

Benny thought about that.

Henry said, "Mr. Morales, is there any way the videos are fake? Did Mrs. Beresford know how to use movie making software?"

Robbie stared at Henry as if he was talking nonsense. "You just saw Walter do the obstacle course with your own eyes. Did that look fake to you?"

"Write that down, Jessie," Benny told his sister. "Walter's not a fake!"

Finished with her questions, Jessie closed her notebook. "It's getting late. Grandfather is coming to pick—" she started when Benny interrupted.

"Can you teach our dog to do tricks?" Benny asked. "Watch is smart, but...maybe not as smart as Walter," he admitted.

Jessie protested. "Watch is super smart."

"I can teach any ankle biter. And I'd be

happy to work with Watch," Robbie told the Aldens. "But, I'm afraid to say, with Mrs. B. gone, I am going to need to find a way to make money. Can you pay for the lessons?"

The children moved aside to talk about it.

"I'll use my allowance," Benny said eagerly. "I want to see Watch do tricks like Pepper and Walter."

Henry thought about it. "I can contribute too. It's a good idea. This way we can come back and investigate what is going on around here."

"We should come back," Jessie said, taping her notebook. "I'll put in my allowance too."

"We need to find out if Walter is really in danger." Violet agreed to add her money.

They went back to Robbie and agreed to set a date for the first lesson.

"How about the middle of next week?" Robbie said. "I'm going to be out of town for a couple days."

"No problem," Henry said.

"I can't wait!" Benny cheered. "This is going to be so much fun!"

Just then Olivia came running out of the

house toward them. "Oh, *there* you are," she said, snatching Walter off the fence. Then she sneezed. Pulling a tissue out of her pocket, she rubbed her nose and told the Aldens, "Your grandfather called. He'll be here to pick you up in a few minutes. You'd better go out front and wait for him."

Jessie wondered why Olivia was in such a hurry to get them to leave. As they walked out the front door, the children saw a police car pull into the circular driveway.

"W-what's happening?" Violet asked.

Olivia wrung her hands. "Mrs. Beresford's prized diamond necklace is missing!"

CHAPTER 5

A Jewel Thief

As soon as they'd come home from their visit to Beresford Mansion, Jessie and Henry tried to find out more about the missing diamond necklace. But after four days they'd found nothing.

"I checked the newspaper again today," Henry said as they sat in the boxcar clubhouse after breakfast. "But still no mention of the theft."

"I looked on the local news websites," said Jessie. "Nothing. And of course, nothing new on Walter's website either."

"I wish we knew what the necklace looked like," Henry said.

Violet, who had been reading in the corner, looked up from her book.

"Oh," she said, pulling a folded white paper from her pocket. "You mean this necklace?" The drawing was a beautiful golden chain with a large pendant. She'd used glitter to make the diamond shine in the sunlight that streamed through the boxcar window.

"How do you know what the necklace looked like?" Jessie asked, leaning in close. "It's gorgeous."

"And very, very valuable," Violet told her sister. "Worth more than a million dollars."

"But how do you know so much about it?" Henry asked. "We looked for hours last night and didn't find anything."

Violet smiled. "Remember when Grandfather picked us up at the mansion, and you and Henry were helping him get our bikes into the van? Well, Benny and I were waiting by the police car. Benny was busy looking at the cool lights on the car. But *I* was busy listening." She winked.

She touched the drawing, knocking a little glitter to the floor. "I overheard the police officers saying Mrs. Beresford owned the Hothouse Diamond. It's famous." She pointed at her art. "I looked it up at the library yesterday while you were reading."

"Clever, Violet," Henry said, tugging on one of her pigtails. "Let's take the drawing with us when we go back to the mansion today."

"You mean for Watch's first lesson with Robbie?" Jessie asked. "That's today?"

Suddenly the door to the boxcar slid open.

"Today's the day!" Benny rushed into the boxcar clubhouse with Watch on a leash.

"I wonder, though," Violet said as she put the drawing back in her pocket. "With everything that is going on at the mansion, what if the lesson is cancelled?"

"It's not," Henry said as he adjusted Watch's collar. "Robbie called last night. He said that his trip was a success and he was back at the guesthouse. And that he can't wait to meet Watch."

***

"Watch is a natural," Robbie told Jessie. "You said he was smart...and he is!"

So far, Robbie had Watch roll over, play dead, and fetch sticks from the yard. Now was time to show him something more difficult.

"Okay, Watch," Robbie took out three small glass vials. "I have hidden a few toys in the yard. Each one has a unique scent. I am going to let you smell a vial, and then you have to get the toy that matches that scent—not one of the others. Can you handle it?"

Watch tipped his head. It seemed as if he understood the directions and was nodding.

Walter was sitting on the fence and Benny thought he saw Walter nod too. "Can Walter do this trick?" Benny asked Robbie.

"He's the best at it." Robbie leaned over and whispered, "Pepper gets distracted and usually brings the wrong thing, but he tries his best. He finds all kinds of treasure in the yard though—from old balls to strange looking rocks."

"Why are you whispering?" Benny asked.

"I don't want Pepper to feel bad about it," Robbie said. "He's sensitive."

Benny put his hand on Pepper's head and said, "Don't worry. You're a smart dog." He then turned his attention to Watch.

Robbie showed Watch a picture of a pink teddy bear. "Dogs are color blind, you know," he told the children.

They knew that.

"They rely on their sense of smell," Jessie said. "This is asking them to single out one particular odor. Police dogs do it all the time. And bloodhounds."

"Did I mention I am also a scientist?" Robbie said. "Add it to my job list. I have been working with dogs and scent-fetching for years. You're right. Some special dogs can do it, but most aren't trained. And often, they are like Pepper—he wants to play rather than do training tasks." He had Benny pick one of the three vials in his hand, let Watch smell it, then took it away. Pointing into the center of the grassy lawn, Robbie commanded, "Fetch!"

Watch bolted forward to the far corner of the yard. He sniffed around some logs.

"Hmmm..." Robbie said. "The toy's not over there." He gave Benny the vial. It smelled like cinnamon.

"Be patient," Jessie said as Watch moved to another area in the yard where there was a small vegetable garden.

"It's not there either," Robbie said. He looked over at Walter. "I know you know where it is. Don't smile at me like that, Crazy Cat!"

"Is he smiling?" Benny asked, looking into Walter's face. The W mark on his brow seemed to wrinkle. "It's hard to tell."

"Oh, he's smiling for sure," Robbie said.

Suddenly, Pepper took off across the yard, past Watch, toward a storage shed near the house. He stopped and started sniffing along the ground, digging with his paws. "He's off the scent!" Robbie said. "That's where I keep my art supplies. I have no idea what that dog is looking for." He turned his attention back to Watch. "My dog's off on his own adventure, but your dog has some woof!" Watch was behind a small patch of roses. "Doggone it! I think he's part bloodhound!"

Watch came bounding back and dropped a cinnamon sweet-smelling pink teddy bear at Jessie's feet.

She leapt forward and hugged him around the neck. "Smart dog!" Jessie cheered. "Good work." She took some dog treats out of her purse. "I knew you could do it!"

"Your dog is a genius!" Robbie agreed. He

quickly took out a second vial. When he took off the lid, Benny said, "Mmmm, bacon!"

"That's Walter's favorite," Robbie said. "I put a bacon cat treat strapped to a plastic toy elephant out there." He waved his hand at the yard. "This should be fast." He started a timer.

After letting Walter smell the vial, the cat disappeared and, less than a minute later, returned with the elephant.

"Walter was faster than Watch," Benny said, stroking the cat's back.

"It was Watch's first time," Jessie said, giving her dog a hug. "He'll do it faster next time!"

"Amazing, right?" Robbie said. "I have no evidence of other cats fetching by scent! I think cats have the reputation of being lazy and that when you let them smell something, they think: you want it, then you get it. But Walter is so different! Walter is a go-getter!"

"That's why he's the Cog!" Benny said.

Just then, Pepper finally came back. He had something shiny in his mouth.

"What did you find?" Robbie said, bending

over to take the item from Pepper. "This isn't one of my toys..." He looked at Benny and whispered, "Pepper needs more practice..."

Pepper dropped the item onto the grass. It was a thick, silver, twisted chain.

"Oh, thanks," Robbie said, quickly scooping the chain off the ground. "I need that." He stuffed it in his pocket.

"It that—?" Henry began, turning to Violet. He wondered if the chain had come from the missing necklace.

"No," she whispered, taking the picture she'd drawn out of her pocket. She traced her finger along the chain that held the Hothouse Diamond. "I got a good look. It's different."

"So," Robbie said, "do you want to see if Watch can do the obstacle course?"

"Yes!" Benny exclaimed, while Jessie, Violet, and Henry exchanged glances.

"Come this way," Robbie said, leading Watch and Benny to the starting place.

Henry and the girls hung back. "That was odd," Henry said. "What do you think that chain was from?"

"I don't know," Jessie replied. "But the

chain was thick enough for a pretty big pendant."

"Is it possible that more of Mrs. Beresford's jewelry is missing?" Violet asked, looking back toward the house.

"Maybe we should ask Geoffrey," Henry said.

"Ask me what?" the deep voice called from across the lawn.

Henry and Jessie went to him, while Violet stayed at the fence to keep an eye on Benny and Watch.

"We were wondering if any more jewelry was missing from the house," Jessie said.

"Ah, good. You're doing your job then," Geoffrey said.

"I don't understand," Jessie said. "You think Walter is in danger, but now there's a thief too. What are we supposed to investigate?"

Geoffrey didn't answer. Instead he said, "The missing items include two rings, a sapphire bracelet, and a ruby pendant on a linked silver chain…" he paused. "The police are still going through Mrs. Beresford's collection, but I am certain that is all." He added, "For now."

"Do you think whoever is taking the jewelry is also out to hurt Walter?" Henry asked.

Geoffrey shrugged. "Solving mysteries is your job—not mine."

Jessie looked at Robbie and thought about how quickly he snatched up the heavy silver chain. "Is Robbie the thief?"

"I don't think this will be so easily solved." Geoffrey pinned his eyes on Jessie. "Wouldn't you agree that right now everyone is a suspect?"

"I suppose," she said, though the man seemed to talk in riddles. "Even you."

He nodded and agreed, "Yes. Even me." Geoffrey then handed Henry an envelope. "I have an invitation for you. Tomorrow night the Funniest Video Association is having a festival at the Regal Theater in Silver City. They're giving Walter an award for Funniest Cat Videos. The award ceremony is a formal affair, and Walter's family and friends are invited. I think you should come. We will all ride in the limousine."

Henry looked around at his siblings. "We

need to ask Grandfather," Henry said. "But we would love to come if we can."

"Good." Geoffrey began to walk away, but Jessie ran to catch up.

"I'm confused," she said. "The other day, at the reading of the will, why did you say Walter *needs* us?" she asked. "Stolen jewelry doesn't hurt Walter. The cousins fighting over the house doesn't hurt him either. And even though WalterTruthTeller has said some mean things online, there haven't been any threats." Shaking her head, she asked, "Is there real evidence that Walter is in danger?"

"Come tomorrow night," Geoffrey said, lowering his eyelids. Jessie could see the sadness there. "That bad feeling in my bones is getting stronger." He pinched his lips together and said, "These old bones don't lie."

CHAPTER 6

Paw Print Photos

The next night Henry, Benny, Violet, and Jessie arrived at the mansion early so they could ride with Walter to the awards show. Grandfather drove them to the big house, then went to the kitchen to have a quick cup of tea with Geoffrey. Meanwhile, the children waited in the foyer with Robbie. Olivia, Natalie, and Matt were coming with them as well, but they were still getting ready.

"I still don't know why Geoffrey was

so insistent that we come along," Jessie whispered to Henry.

Henry nodded. "I know. But it's fun to be part of the excitement."

Olivia seemed to be running late. "I can't find my medication," she moaned, sniffling. "I think I am getting a cold." She was wearing a mustard-colored dress that swept over one shoulder and reached to the floor. Her little matching purse was stuffed with tissues.

"Maybe you should stay here," Robbie told her.

It was clear to the children that Robbie didn't care for Olivia much, and the feeling was mutual.

"If you're worried about catching my cold, maybe *you* should stay back," she said, punctuating the thought with a loud sneeze.

"Ugh," he said. "Get a mask."

"Get a life," she retorted. She turned toward the grand staircase and called for Walter. "Come!"

Violet couldn't help but notice that Olivia was wearing a large blue sapphire necklace. "It doesn't take an artist to know that pendant clashes with her dress," she told Jessie in a whisper. "Olivia seems very fashion conscious. I'd have thought she'd pick something with bits of yellow, like topaz maybe."

"I bet it's real…isn't it?" Jessie said.

Suddenly Natalie burst into the foyer, followed by Matt.

"You took it!" Natalie shouted, pointing at Olivia. She marched up to her cousin, high heels clacking on the marble floor, and grabbed the necklace.

Olivia coughed. "Stop it! You're choking me."

Natalie was wearing a blue dress. Violet was certain she picked it to match the sapphire necklace.

"That's my *aunt's* pendant and I was going to wear it tonight—you…you…thief!" She tightened her hands around the necklace. Olivia gasped for air.

"Whoa. That's enough, Natalie." Matt broke up the battle by dragging his sister away. "First, you can't make accusations while the police are investigating missing jewelry. And second, if you choke Olivia to death, you'll go to jail."

"And then you'll miss the awards show," Benny added.

Natalie turned to glare at him.

Matt pointed a finger straight at his sister. "You need to lighten up, Natalie. I also lost everything when that will was read. But Auntie Beulah's wishes are set. Nothing more to do about it. Go on, borrow another of Auntie's jewels from Walter. I'm sure he won't mind if you wear a necklace tonight. We will wait."

"I wanted *that* necklace..." she said, growling at Olivia and muttering, "thief!"

"It all belongs to Walter now," Olivia retorted, "And borrowing a necklace for the evening from my favorite cat does not make me a thief." She turned to Matt. "Thanks for helping. Everyone around here acts like I am the bad guy. All I have done is to take care of the cat. In the will, I was rewarded for my good work. I'm not evil."

"I'm not so sure." He shook his head. "I'm still on Natalie's side, but I just didn't want her to strangle you."

Olivia huffed. "Well, I am on Walter's

side." She gave a small smile. "Auntie Beulah gave me a job, and no matter what you and your sister think, I will do it. I am not a thief. I love this cat and I deserve everything I have been given." With that she sneezed again.

She walked over to the staircase and called for Walter again. "Come," she said, in the same tone of voice Robbie used.

At the sound of the command, Walter slipped quietly down the steps, stopping at Olivia's feet and sitting at attention.

"Just like I taught him," Robbie told Henry.

Olivia bent and placed a diamond-studded collar on the cat. The stones glittered, creating little rainbows along the walls and floor.

"Now we're all dressed up," murmured Jessie. She and Violet were wearing their favorite party dresses, and Henry and Benny were wearing their best shirts. Benny was even wearing a tie. Watch, who was waiting in the limousine, had been given a bath and was wearing a fresh collar.

"Well, then," Olivia said. The fabric of her dress crinkled as she headed to the door. "Time to go."

***

When the limousine reached the Regal Theater, the children could see a red carpet had been laid out front, all the way to the curb. A small crowd of fans had gathered on the sidewalk, and there were even reporters with cameras. Usually Violet didn't like crowds, but she was relieved to get to the theater, since the whole ride had been awkwardly silent. Nobody from Beresford Mansion—Natalie, Matt, Olivia, and Robbie—had said a word to one another.

Geoffrey steered the limousine over to the curb and pulled up to the edge of the red carpet. "Walter will get out first," he told the others. "With Olivia."

At that, Natalie sighed loudly. It was the first sound she'd made since the ride had started.

"Members of Walter's fan club will be here," Geoffrey explained. He handed Benny an envelope. "Pass these out to anyone who wants one," he instructed. "We do this at every event. I make it my responsibility to make sure that no fan goes home without a paw-printed picture."

As he turned, Jessie noticed that there was a bit of purple coloring on Geoffrey's fingers. It could have come from anywhere, she figured, but then again, it was a good idea to pay attention to everything. She made a mental note to write it down in the notebook in her purse. After all, the night couldn't be all fun, not when there was a mystery to solve.

When the door to the limousine opened, Watch pushed Walter aside and leapt out of the car.

"Watch!" Jessie scolded. She wished she'd thought to hold on to him.

Then Walter darted out, with Olivia struggling to catch him. But by then Walter and Watch were rolling playfully around on the red carpet together, having fun while the reporters' cameras clicked away.

The children got out of the limousine next, followed by the other adults. Olivia shooed Walter away from Watch and called for him to follow her down the red carpet. Meanwhile Jessie made sure Watch didn't stray from the red carpet.

"Is that your dog?" a reporter asked Henry. "He's so funny! What's his name?"

"Watch," Benny answered. "But tonight is Walter's special night," he said to the reporter. "Watch is just here as his friend."

As the reporter began to write down Watch's name, Benny remembered the photos Geoffrey had given him to hand out. He held out the package of photos. "Want a signed picture?"

"I'd love one," the reporter said.

Benny opened the envelope and started to hand a picture to the reporter, when he suddenly stopped. The paw print signature was in purple ink, but so was a hand-written message scrawled across the top of every picture:

> *WALTER IS A FAKE*
> *—WalterTruthTeller*

Henry reached over and grabbed the picture from Benny. "Sorry about that," he said to the reporter. "We'll get some new photos and be right back."

Henry and Benny hurried over to Geoffrey as he was climbing back into the driver's seat of the limousine. "I just need to park the car, and I'll be back in a minute," he said.

"We need to talk to you now," Henry said, showing the chauffeur the marked-up photos. "What happened to these?"

Geoffrey looked surprised. "I...I don't know," he said. His face fell as he flipped through the stack of photos. "But they are all ruined!" He sighed.

"Whoever did it used the same color ink as the paw prints," Henry noted.

"And the same color ink you have on your hands," Benny said, pointing at Geoffrey's fingers.

Geoffrey shook his head. "You don't think I'm WalterTruthTeller, do you?"

Benny and Henry looked at each other. They didn't know what to say. They wanted to believe Geoffrey.

"I made the cat paw prints with a special rubber stamp and purple ink," Geoffrey went on. "You don't think that Walter sat around and stamped hundreds of photos with his paw, do you? Someone must have written on the pictures after I finished."

"Maybe we should look for a purple marker?" Benny whispered to Henry.

"I guess so," Henry agreed.

Geoffrey put the envelope of photos back in the glove compartment of the car. "I hate to disappoint Walter's fans, but we can't give these out tonight." He sighed again. "I knew something was going to happen! I'll tell you this…these photos are just the beginning!"

CHAPTER 7

The Funniest Cat

Inside the Regal Theater, Jessie and Henry were led by an usher to their reserved seats in the front row. Benny and Violet had gone backstage with Walter, Watch, the cousins, and Robbie.

"I just wanted to be away from the Beresford cousins," Jessie told Henry. "There's so much fighting, I can't make sense of anything."

"It is crazy, isn't it?" Henry replied. "We seem to have two mysteries going at the same time."

"Three, I think," Jessie said, sitting back in the plush red velvet chair and taking out her notebook. "One, Geoffrey thinks someone is out to hurt Walter. Two, WalterTruthTeller is trying to ruin Walter's reputation. And three..."

Henry filled that one in. "Expensive jewelry is missing from Mrs. Beresford's home."

Jessie tapped her pen on a blank page. "I think it's all connected, but I don't know how yet."

"Do you think if we find the thief, it'll be the same person as WalterTruthTeller and whoever Geoffrey wants us to look out for?"

Jessie shrugged and rubbed her forehead. This mystery seemed so complicated. All the pieces were giving her a headache. "I hope so," she said at last. "I mean, everyone is a suspect for every crime. Natalie and Matt hate the cat. They want money, so why not just take jewels and sell them? It wouldn't be as much as the house, but I bet there are several millions of dollars worth of stones already missing. With a few other pieces, they'd have so much money."

"Then there's Olivia. Olivia loves the cat and gets the benefit of the inheritance—the house isn't hers but she lives like a queen," Henry said. "Why would she want to ruin Walter's reputation? Or steal jewels?"

"I don't know," Jessie said. "But no one seems to trust her. Not Matt, Natalie, or Robbie, so we need to find out more." She jotted Olivia's name down under Matt and Natalie.

"What about Robbie?" Henry asked.

"He does seem to need money," Jessie said. "The only reason he's still at the house is that he trains Walter. No one wants to buy his art, so maybe he is stealing jewels to buy art supplies and food?"

"There was that silver chain in the yard," Henry added. "Which he pocketed."

"Good point." Jessie nodded and wrote in her notebook. Then she looked up, chewing her pen. "Now the only one left to think about is Geoffrey." She wrote his name down and underlined it. "How does he know something bad might happen to Walter?"

"He's guessing, because the will left

everything to Walter," Henry said. "And he said he has that feeling in his bones. But he really seems to want to help Walter."

Jessie shook her head. "But maybe that's only because if something happened to Walter, Geoffrey is out of a place to live and a job."

"That's true," Henry said.

"Or maybe he's going to get rid of Walter himself, then go live somewhere fancy with money from selling the necklaces. He'd be so rich, he'd never have to work again," Jessie said, then paused. "I just realized something odd. Geoffrey said that two rings and a sapphire bracelet were stolen too...how did he know exactly what items of jewelry were taken?"

"That is strange," Henry said. "Plus the ink on his fingers makes me wonder if he is WalterTruthTeller."

"What do you mean?" Jessie asked.

"If Walter isn't famous anymore, then nobody will notice if he ends up back at the cat shelter. Then Geoffrey could sneak away in the night, sell the necklaces and rings, and go buy that island he mentioned!"

Jessie wasn't so fast to agree. "I am not sure Geoffrey is the one we are looking for," she said as the music began and the lights dimmed.

Suddenly, Violet and Benny rushed down the aisle and plopped into their seats. The cousins and Robbie had stayed with Walter backstage.

"I met so many famous cats backstage!" Benny said, bouncing with excitement. "There was one that plays piano, and one that paints, and one that surfs…"

"And a whole cat band!" Violet added. "We left Watch backstage with Robbie," she added. "He growled a little when I tried to bring him out here."

"Watch and Walter are BPFF," Benny said. "Best Pet Friends Forever!" He laughed.

After a short welcome by the president of the Funniest Video Association, a video began on the screen. "It's a new Walter video!" Benny was so excited. "I've seen them all, but I can tell from the beginning—I've never seen this one!"

Violet leaned over to Jessie. "I have a bad

feeling. There can't be any new ones! Who made it?"

"Maybe Mrs. Beresford made it before she died?" Jessie said, but a second later it was clear this was no ordinary video.

The opening scene was from the day the Aldens had their lesson with Robbie. Watch had been cut out, but there was footage of Walter sniffing the scent of the toy and then fetching it from the yard.

Then a voice boomed…*"Impossible!"* The

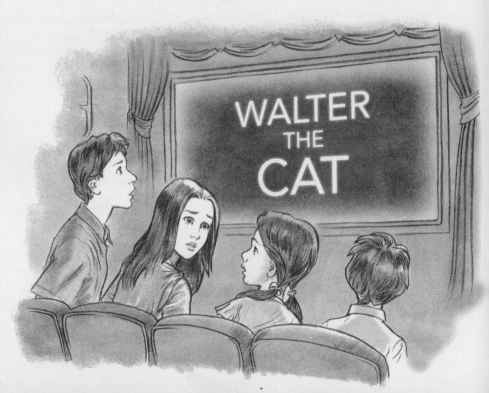

voice had been disguised by a computer so it didn't sound like a man's voice or a woman's. It was rough and harsh and deep. "It is impossible that a cat can fetch something so far away from a scent. Dogs fetch. Cats don't! Not even Walter can do that!"

The video changed to show a green screen, the kind used to film special effects, and a cutout photo of Walter with a toy in his mouth dancing across it like a cartoon. The audience gasped.

"That's not fair," Jessie said under her breath. "We saw him fetch that toy for real." The video was trying to make it seem like Walter's trick was only a fake special effect.

"There was no fetch," the video said. "You've all been tricked. WalterTruthTeller tells the truth."

Benny jumped up in his seat. "It happened! We can prove it!"

Before Henry could stop him, Benny had rushed backstage. Someone had turned the video off, and the lights went up.

A few moments later, Benny was standing in front of the screen holding Walter in his arms.

"I don't know why anyone would say those terrible things about Walter," Benny told the crowd. "He does all his own tricks! I saw him with my own eyes."

Robbie came out onto the stage and joined Benny. He looked over at Violet, Jessie, and Henry in the front row. "How are we going to do this? I'm not prepared." The trainer looked panicked. "I'm in the dog pound here."

"I know what to do," Violet said softly. "Jessie, do you have perfume in your purse?"

"No," Jessie said. "But Natalie is standing near the bottom of the stage. I bet she might."

"She and Matt seemed to be as shocked as the rest of us," Henry said.

Jessie noted their expressions. It certainly didn't look like either of them knew about the video. In fact, Natalie looked so angry that Jessie thought that maybe sending Violet over there was a bad idea.

"It's okay," Violet said. "I'll tell her I'm going to help."

Violet went to Natalie and sure enough, she had perfume. She delivered it to Robbie and explained her idea.

His eyes lit up as he said, "Benny, take Walter offstage and make sure he can't see the audience."

Robbie then took the perfume into the crowd and asked a man for his wallet. He put a few drops of the perfume on the wallet, then put the wallet in his wife's purse. "Leave it unzipped," Robbie requested. He laughed, saying, "I haven't trained him to open zippers yet, though I bet he could!"

Robbie returned to the stage and Benny brought Walter back out. "Who is wearing perfume?" he asked the crowd. "Or cologne." A lot of hands went up. "If you have some in your bag, please open the vial. Let's make this as confusing as possible for Walter." He chuckled as he looked at Violet and said, "I hope no one here has the same scent as Natalie."

Robbie let Walter sniff Natalie's perfume, then Benny set him down. At first it seemed that WalterTruthTeller might be right. The cat stretched and lay down on the stage.

"Cats sleep 70 percent of the day," Jessie said. "Let's hope that's not Walter's plan."

Robbie gave a loud-awkward laugh.

"Walter's so charming. He thinks he's being funny! Mrs. Beresford would cut out his playful defiance when she posted the videos online." He said to Walter, "What's funny at home is not so funny right now. Get up."

Walter just rolled over.

Robbie looked even more nervous. It was clear he was worried that Walter wasn't going to play along.

Just then a bark came from backstage.

"It's Watch!" Henry whispered to Jessie.

Watch barked again, and Walter got up. Watch barked once more, and Benny ran offstage to get the dog.

"I think Watch is encouraging Walter!" Jessie said. Sure enough, Watch came onstage and pushed Walter with his nose. They two of them were putting on their own show, and the audience cheered. Benny stood in the stage wings and cheered too.

Suddenly Walter jumped off the stage. He crept into the audience, slipping under seats, crawling over arm rests...until he found the wallet and brought it back to Robbie, carrying it in his mouth.

"He did it!" Violet squealed.

The crowd went wild. Cameras snapped photos and some people had their videos recording.

Watch went back over to where Benny waited in the wings. It seemed as if he knew it was time to give Walter the spotlight. Or maybe he was just tired from the excitement. "Good dog," Benny said, giving his head a scratch.

Meanwhile Walter had brought the wallet up to the stage. He made a sound like a barking dog, lay down, and started chewing on the leather.

Robbie snatched up the wallet and held it high. Walter leapt for it a few times on his back legs, then lay back down in snoozing position, curled in a ball on the stage.

"Whoever WalterTruthTeller is, you now know the truth...Walter is the real deal!" Robbie shouted.

The audience burst into applause. Robbie returned the wallet to the owner, then climbed back onstage amid a standing ovation for Walter. "I trained him," Robbie announced proudly. "A lot of puppy love goes into every thing that cat does. You can call me and get an appointment for your own dog or cat. I'm in business!"

The applause continued as Olivia took the stage to accept Walter's Funniest Cat Trophy. As she accepted the award, the children went backstage to look for Watch and Benny. When they found the two of them, Watch was drinking from a water bowl with Walter's name on it.

"Good job, Watch," Violet said.

"Seems like the night is a success," Henry said.

"It sure is," Jessie said. She couldn't tell the others until they were alone, but now she was sure that Robbie was the jewel thief. He had just revealed his trick to stealing the jewels!

Chapter 8

The Cat Burglar

The fighting started in the limousine on the way back to the Beresford mansion. Olivia was carrying the big "Funniest Cat" trophy and Natalie wanted it.

"I'd like to have it for sentimental reasons," she told Olivia. "Since you stay at the house with Walter, it's only fair that I get to display the trophy at my apartment."

"You're ridiculous." Olivia pulled the trophy away and shoved it behind her back. She had to lean forward, but the trophy was hidden in the folds of her coat. "The trophy belongs to Walter and everything that belongs to Walter is in my care."

"No, you're the ridiculous one," Natalie countered. "I don't think you even like that cat!"

"You're the one who wants to get rid of him!" Olivia shrieked.

Matt rolled his eyes. "You are both acting like children. You should play rock, paper, scissors for the trophy. Winner gets it. Best out of three?" He made his hand like scissors.

"*Now* look who's being ridiculous!" his sister shouted.

Benny leaned in. "I like rock, paper, scissors," he told Matt. "If they don't want to play with you, I will."

Matt grinned. "I'm glad to have you along, Benny. You make everything more fun."

"You know what would be really fun?" Benny asked. "Taking the limousine through the drive-through window of the ice-cream shop so we could get cones! I bet Walter would love ice cream."

Jessie started to protest. It was late and they needed to talk to Robbie alone and solve the jewelry mystery. Maybe they'd get lucky and find out he was WalterTruthTeller too.

"I don't think—" she began.

Natalie interrupted. "I believe ice cream is a *wonderful* idea," she said, then asked Geoffrey to make the stop. "I bet that Walter loves ice cream." She put her hand on Walter's head. He was sitting between Olivia and the window.

"Sugar is not good for cats," Olivia countered.

"Watch likes ice cream," Benny said, petting Watch's belly. "It's delicious for everyone."

Olivia sighed. "Fine. Just a small cone for Walter." Reaching into her bag, Olivia took out a tissue and sneezed. As she put the tissue back, a small bag of cat treats fell to the floor.

Jessie snatched up the bag to keep Watch and Walter from snagging the treats first. A few fell out and Jessie picked them up one by one. Her fingers smelled like bacon.

Olivia gave her a clean tissue to wipe them off.

"Thanks," Olivia told Jessie. "I keep the

treats for Walter just in case he ever runs off.
He will do anything for one of these snacks."
She patted the bag.

"I'll do anything for snacks too," Benny
said. "I think Walter and I are very much
alike!"

Everyone chuckled and the rest of the
car ride was filled with ice-cream cones and
friendly conversation. Robbie was talking
with Olivia about a book they'd both read.
No one was fighting.

"Let's stop off at the mansion," Jessie told
her siblings. "I have to tell you something."
Once she told the others what she suspected
about Robbie, maybe they could confront him
tonight. Then the case would be closed—or
one of the cases at least.

Benny sighed. "My tummy's full and I'm
tired." He took off his tie and put it in his
coat pocket.

"It's just one more stop," Jessie said.

***

"Why are we here again?" Henry asked, as
they stood in front of the guesthouse where
Robbie lived. Robbie had gone inside.

"Robbie's the thief," Jessie said. "I'm sure of it. He needs money. He didn't get anything in the will, so it makes sense he's stealing. He went on a trip for a few days right after the jewels were taken…"

"Maybe to sell them?" Henry said.

"There *was* a chain in the grass in his yard that matched the description of the ruby chain," Violet said. But she didn't sound convinced.

"And he is the one who taught Walter to fetch!" Jessie insisted. "I think Walter is fetching the jewels and bringing them to Robbie."

"But…how?" Henry asked, squinting his eyes. "I mean he would have to train Walter to steal each piece. He would have to sneak into the house and put something stinky on the necklaces, then take it back to the guesthouse and let Walter smell them, *then* put the jewels back, and *then* send Walter to get them."

"Right!" Jessie said.

"But why wouldn't Robbie just *take* the jewelry?" Violet asked.

"Yeah!" Benny added, "It's a lot more trouble to take the jewelry and then put it back!"

"Maybe...maybe he didn't want to leave fingerprints," Jessie said. But she knew her idea about Robbie using Walter to steal jewels just didn't make sense. "I guess you're right. But...what about the silver chain? That's the only detail that doesn't have an explanation."

"Oh!" Violet said. "He said his easel was broken and was missing one of those little chains that hold up the side. I think the chain that Pepper found was for the easel, not a necklace."

"I suppose you're right about that too." Jessie admitted. "So it looks like Robbie can't be the thief." She sighed. "I thought we had it all figured out, but it looks like we are back to the beginning!"

Henry counted the remaining suspects. "Natalie, Matt, Olivia, and Geoffrey—who is taking the jewels?"

Violet scratched her chin. "I think we should look at the mystery a different way. All this time we've been searching for the jewel thief.

Let's look for WalterTruthTeller instead." She nodded her head slowly. "If we figure out who is trying to prove Walter is a fake and why, I bet we will solve this entire mystery!"

CHAPTER 9

Walter Truth Teller

Saturday morning was Watch's last lesson with Robbie.

"We are all out of allowance," Benny said, sitting on the fence so he could see Watch jump through hoops. "I'm sad." He glumly began to unwrap a cheese stick that he had brought as snack.

"I'll take over the training," Jessie said. "I've been watching some dog training videos on the Internet and think I can get Watch to do some amazing things."

"Can we record him doing them?" Benny asked. "We could start our own video channel—Watch could be famous like Walter!"

Henry laughed. "It's a lot of work to have a famous dog...who will run the fan club?"

"Me!" Violet said. "I'll design the T-shirts and we could have posters."

"Maybe Grandfather could buy a limo to drive us around?" Benny suggested. "That would be amazing!" He waved around the piece of cheese he was holding.

Henry laughed even harder. "I'm sure he'll want to do that. We'll get him a hat like Geoffrey's."

"Since it's our last lesson day here at the mansion," Violet said, "we need to find out who WalterTruthTeller is."

"I've been thinking," Jessie said. "What makes us all so sure that WalterTruthTeller is here at the Beresford house? We keep going back to the same suspects, but maybe it's just some mean person with a laptop wanting to cause trouble. The Internet is full of those."

"The fan club pictures were ruined," Benny said. "Someone in the house had to have done that."

"And the video at the awards ceremony was filmed here," Violet added. "I didn't see anyone else around. But all the cousins and Geoffrey were at the house when it was made."

"So it must be one of them," Jessie agreed. "What do we do next?"

"Oof!" Suddenly Benny fell off the fence into Robbie's yard. He giggled as Walter snatched the cheese out of his hand and ran away. "Sneaky cat!" he shouted. "Come back with my snack!" He dusted off his jeans as the cat disappeared around the back of the house.

"That cat!" He looked at Jessie. "Maybe he is taking the jewels! He sure is clever."

"But who is he giving them to?" Henry let out a frustrated sigh.

Just then they heard someone shouting from the house.

"It's gone!" Geoffrey yelled. "All gone! Help!"

The Aldens looked at one another.

"What's gone?" Violet asked. "The jewelry?"

"All of it?" Benny wondered. He could still see Walter across the lawn.

Jessie turned to Robbie, who was just finishing up the lesson with Watch. "We should go see what that's about. Can you keep Watch a little longer? I mean, just as a favor?"

Robbie paused for a moment. "You can't pay me extra, can you?"

Henry and Jessie shook their heads no.

Suddenly Robbie smiled. "That's all right. I heard you all talking outside my window last night. I'm glad I'm not a suspect anymore." He pointed at the house. "Go and find WalterTruthTeller before he—or she—ruins my reputation!"

***

Geoffrey was waiting for the Aldens just outside the house.

"What's going on?" Henry asked.

"Is there more missing jewelry?" Jessie added.

"Yes, and there's more," Geoffrey said. "Here, I'll show you." He led them to a side door on the house, covered by vines. There was a keypad next to the door. Geoffrey entered a code and the door swung open. He flicked on the lights to reveal a small basement office.

"What's this?" Violet asked.

"It was my secret," Geoffrey replied. "Until now."

The children stood at the doorway and peered inside. In the small room was a powerful computer, boxes of papers, and a printing press for T-shirts.

"Do you understand now?" Geoffrey asked.

"I think so," Henry said. "You're president of the Cog Fan Club, aren't you?"

Benny could see the T-shirt press was used to make shirts like the one he owned. He also noticed purple ink fingerprints on the side of one of the boxes, which he was sure held the stamped photos of Walter.

"I never told Mrs. Beresford what I was doing," Geoffrey explained. "This room, and everything in it, was my secret. She was so proud of Walter and I wanted to do something nice for them."

"I love my magazine and T-shirt," Benny said. "Thank you for being president!"

"I gave all the money the club earned to the shelter, just like Mrs. Beresford would have wanted," he said. "She was such a lovely woman—I just don't understand why anyone would want to ruin Walter's reputation online."

Jessie felt a chill. "Did WalterTruthTeller strike again?"

"What did he say now?" Henry asked.

"It's worse than that." Geoffrey sat down at his computer and logged in. "Everything is gone. Mrs. Beresford's videos, the fan club website, everything! It's like Walter no longer exists online." He looked frantically at the screen, clicking the mouse and shaking his head. "I knew something bad was going to happen! I told you my bones never lie!"

"Someone must have hacked your system," Jessie said.

"Do Matt or Natalie know computers well enough to do this?" Henry asked. "It would take an expert to get it done."

"Whoever broke in and deleted everything left a note." Geoffrey clicked to the Cog Fan

Club website. In place of the usual links to videos and merchandise was a banner that read:

> *Good-bye*
> *—WalterTruthTeller*

"Your videos are not the only thing now missing," Jessie said. "We better hurry to the house, because…I have a feeling that Olivia is now missing too!"

CHAPTER 10

The Clues Add Up

Jessie was right—Olivia was gone!

Her room in the mansion was empty, with all her clothes and things cleared out.

Henry emptied the contents of her wastebasket onto the floor. "Cat treats," he said, setting the plastic treat bag on the desk.

"She must have used them to get Walter to steal the jewelry," Violet said.

"Look at this!" Jessie said. She held up the Funniest Cat trophy. "Olivia left it lying on its side in the closet. Natalie was right all along. Olivia never liked Walter."

"It's worse than that," Henry said, holding out an empty medicine bottle. "She was allergic to cats."

"That explains the sneezing," Jessie said. "She wasn't actually getting a cold. The truth was that she couldn't find her medication so she started sneezing around Walter."

"Do you remember when Olivia told Natalie that she had 'talents'? She said it during a fight, but I didn't think anything of it then." Jessie pulled out her notebook. "I didn't even write that down, but maybe she meant she had computer hacking talents."

"Why would Olivia do this?" Geoffrey asked. "I just don't understand. She had a great life here. Watching Walter isn't so hard and the benefits are wonderful."

"We had a list of reasons we thought you might be WalterTruthTeller," Jessie admitted, turning to that page in her notebook. "I think these motivations all apply to Olivia." She read from the list: 'Get Walter off the Internet and let the fame fade away so no one notices when he is put into a shelter, then sell the jewels.'"

She looked up. "And you did say you wanted to go buy an island."

"I don't really want an island," Geoffrey said sadly. "I didn't mean it. I was just annoyed by the cousins. You know, I love this house and that cat."

"We know that now," Jessie told him.

"I'm glad you aren't the thief," Benny told Geoffrey. "Or WalterTruthTeller."

"Me too," Geoffrey said. He then added, "But Olivia didn't wait until Walter's fame faded away. If Walter wasn't famous anymore, she might have been able to take the jewels and sneak off like a cat in the night."

"I think she got impatient," Jessie said. "No one believed Walter's tricks were fake—especially not after Robbie's training show at the awards ceremony." She picked up the trophy and said, "Olivia just decided to hack the system, remove all traces of Walter, and run away."

"I knew something was up. My bones started rattling the instant I saw WalterTruthTeller appear in the comments for the fan club," Geoffrey said. "Then you came along..." he glanced from Henry and Benny to the girls. "I was so glad that you were here to help." He sighed. "And now we know the real truth behind everything!"

"What do we do now?" Benny asked the others. "Olivia ran away!"

"We call the police," Henry said. "We tell them what we know and we let them find her."

***

At home later that afternoon Henry hung up the phone and turned to his siblings.

"That was Geoffrey and Robbie," he said. "Geoffrey said the police arrested Olivia at the airport. She had a bag full of jewels—it turned out she'd been taking them for years, using Walter."

"So I was *sort of* right about Walter being trained to steal the jewels," Jessie said. "Only I was wrong about Robbie doing the training."

Henry nodded. "Robbie hadn't really been the one to teach Walter to fetch. Olivia had taught him that trick herself and perfected it. Robbie said he'd always wondered why Walter was so good at fetching. It's because Walter already knew how."

***

Jessie leaned back in her chair at her boxcar desk. It was Sunday. The door to the boxcar opened with a bang and Benny climbed inside, popcorn bowl in hand. Watch was behind him, snatching up the stray kernels that dropped.

"Is there a new cog video?" Benny asked, setting down the bowl and tugging over a beanbag chair. He set it up in the perfect spot to see the computer screen.

"Yes," Jessie said. "But shouldn't we wait for the others?"

The door opened again, and in came Violet and Henry, along with Natalie and Matt.

"We heard that Sundays are special around here," Natalie said. She set down a chocolate cake with a photo of Walter etched into the frosting.

"Cake!" Benny cheered. "It's Cog Cake! That should be extra delicious!"

"I have the plates!" Matt said.

Geoffrey came in carrying Walter. "And I have the cat!"

Benny jumped off his beanbag, spilling popcorn. "It's a party!" he cheered.

Everyone laughed.

"Geoffrey will be keeping Walter and living in Mrs. Beresford's house from now on," Natalie told everyone.

"I thought you wanted to get rid of Walter," Jessie said. "We heard you say it."

"I did," Natalie admitted. "Matt and I had these big business plans to start a children's theater company in the house and we were worried that kids who have cat allergies might not be able to come."

"I was going to manage the company from Robbie's guesthouse," Matt said. "But now, Robbie is staying there for as long as he wants. His trip was to see an art dealer in New York that specializes in cat art. I'm betting that someday, he's going to be very famous."

"Not as famous as Walter," Benny said, picking up the cat and petting him.

Walter barked like a dog. Watch barked too.

"Robbie would have come tonight but he is working on a painting," Matt said. He turned to Violet. "He says you should come over and paint with him. Pepper found the missing chain in the yard, so he finally fixed his easel."

"I'd love to!" Violet agreed enthusiastically.

Jessie loaded the newest cat video. Now there were words below the title stating the video was taken by Robbie and posted by the Cog Fan Club. Jessie turned to Geoffrey and smiled.

"I've been busy," he said with a shrug. "I have a new job as videographer." He smiled. "Plus, I'm the cat nanny!" He added with a wink, "Don't ever call me a babysitter!"

Jessie smiled warmly at Geoffrey, then turned to Matt and Natalie. "What happened with the theater you wanted to start?"

"We met with Mrs. Hudson, the lawyer," Matt said. "As long as we all agreed, she said we could make a few changes to the will that fit with Auntie's wishes. So, we all decided to sell off Walter's boat, some of the jewels, and a few other things—"

"Not the limo!" Benny protested. "Please, say not the limo! I love riding in that car!"

Natalie laughed. "We kept the limo because kids will love it at our school too."

She said, "The land behind the house is big enough that we are going to build a special school building, with apartments above it for me and Matt."

"Walter and Geoffrey get the main house," Matt started, when Geoffrey chimed in.

"It's too big," Geoffrey told them. "I am going to build a wall to make it two halves and the animal shelter is going to move in with me. Robbie, when he's not creating great art, has been hired to train the strays—so when they are adopted, they can do tricks!"

Henry flopped back into a beanbag chair. "It all worked out. The best for Walter and the best for everyone."

"Just like Mrs. Beresford would have wanted," Geoffrey said, gathering Walter on his lap. "I've got nothing but good feelings now in these old bones."

Jessie snuggled up with Watch, and Violet sliced the cake. Benny got the biggest piece. It was a corner with a picture of Walter's whole left ear on it. "I wish we could have Cog Cake every Sunday night," Benny said, dipping his finger and licking off the frosting.

"Instead of popcorn?" Henry asked.

"Oh no," Benny said, shaking his head. "Maybe we can have both?!"

"We will see..." Grandfather said as he joined everyone. "Now pass me the popcorn, please."

Benny took a big handful before handing over the bowl.

When they were all settled, Jessie pressed play—and the newest Walter the Cat video began.

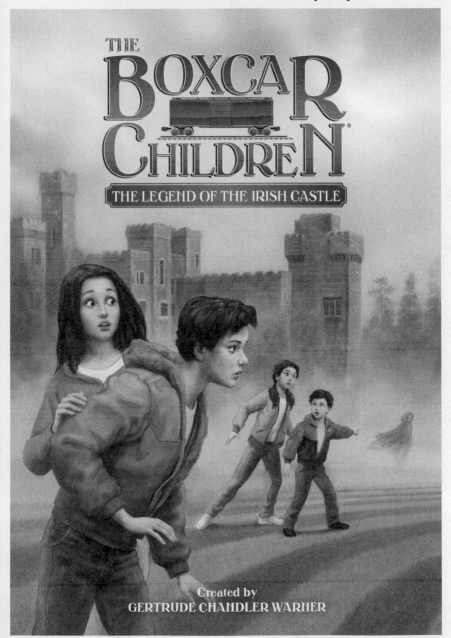

CHAPTER 1

The Bad Omen

Henry Alden pushed a cart full of luggage through the bustling airport of Dublin, Ireland. All around him, people were walking very fast and pulling large suitcases. A pilot and two flight attendants wearing navy blue uniforms passed by, their shoes clicking on the tile floor. On the public address system, a voice said, "Last call for flight two-seventeen!" Airports always made the Alden children feel very excited. They loved traveling to new places.

"I wonder how long it will take to get to the castle," said twelve-year-old Jessie Alden. She looked at her watch and reset it to the local time, six hours later than in their home in Greenfield. Between the time change and the long flight, the children were feeling tired. But they had been looking forward to their vacation in Ireland for a long time and couldn't wait to explore the castles and the beautiful countryside.

Grandfather glanced at the map in his hand. "According to the map, it should take about two hours to get to where we're staying."

Grandfather was also carrying Benny, who at six was the youngest Alden. Benny had been asleep when the plane landed and was just starting to wake up. His head rested on Grandfather's shoulder. "Erin, the owner of the castle, said she would pick us up right outside the airport."

Ten-year-old Violet walked ahead of the other children and snapped a picture of a sign that read "This Way to Dublin" with an arrow pointing toward the doors. Violet was planning to make a scrapbook of this adventure when the Aldens returned home, and she thought a picture of the sign would be perfect for the cover.

The automatic doors opened with a *whoosh*, and the Aldens walked out into the sunshine. Taxis were lined up along the curb.

"What a beautiful day!" Violet said, snapping another picture.

"We're lucky the sun is out," Henry said. "I've read that it rains a lot in Ireland."

"We don't mind a little rain," said Violet. She took off her purple sweater and tied it around her waist. "We always found fun things to do on rainy days when we lived in the boxcar!"

After their parents died, the Alden children had run away. They were afraid of their grandfather because they thought he was mean and they wouldn't like living with him. In the woods, the children had found an abandoned boxcar and made it their home. They had lots of adventures, and even found their dog, Watch, in the woods. He became part of their family too. When their grandfather found them, they realized he wasn't mean at all.

Grandfather Alden took the children to his home to live with him and his housekeeper, Mrs. McGregor. Grandfather brought the boxcar to his home, and put it in the backyard to use as a clubhouse.

"That must be our ride," Jessie said, pointing to a white van that said "Duncarraig Castle" in green letters on the side.

Grandfather and the children walked toward the van just as a woman got out. She had a long red braid that hung down over her shoulder. "Céad míle fáilte!" she said. "That means 'a hundred thousand welcomes.' I'm Erin."

The children introduced themselves, and Henry and Erin loaded the luggage into the van. Grandfather helped Benny get buckled in. Benny tried to wake himself up, but as soon as they started driving, he closed his eyes again.

"Poor Benny," said Violet. "He seems so tired."

"You all must be tired after that long trip," Erin said. "And hungry too. Let's stop for lunch when we get to Howth."

Benny sat up and opened his eyes. "Did someone say 'lunch'?"

Everyone laughed. "I thought lunch might wake you up," Grandfather said.

Erin took the scenic route toward the seaside village of Howth. The tall cliffs alongside the road were bright green and towered over the ocean below. White seagulls sailed through the air hunting for fish. Erin told the children about the sights. "Down there is Dublin Bay," she said, pointing to the water. "And that's Baily Lighthouse."

She pointed to a narrow white building perched on the edge of a cliff. It was a steep drop down to the ocean, where the waves crashed against the rocks.

Erin continued. "The village of Howth has been a busy fishing port for hundreds of years, but the fog can make it dangerous. The lighthouse shines to warn the boats when they are getting too close to these cliffs."

Violet shivered thinking about how scary a shipwreck would be. "I'm so glad we traveled by plane instead of boat!" she said.

"I think a ship would be exciting!" Henry said. He was fourteen and liked adventure. "As long as the captain knew what he was doing."

"Don't worry, Violet," Grandfather said. "Ships don't rely on lighthouses anymore. Now they use computers to navigate the ocean, so sailors always know when they are close to land."

Erin parked the van in front of a row of very old buildings painted bright colors. "Let's have lunch on the pier. How do you feel about fish and chips?" she asked Benny.

Grandfather explained, "In Ireland, chips are what we think of as french fries back in the U.S. Fish and chips is a dish of fried fish with fried potatoes on the side."

Benny rubbed his stomach. "I don't mind if they call them fries or chips, as long as they come with ketchup!"

The Aldens sat down at a table covered in a red-checkered cloth, and Erin ordered their food. From where they sat they could watch the boats coming in and out of port. Some raised big nets full of fish onto the pier.

While the Aldens and Erin waited for their food, Jessie pulled out the book she had been reading on the plane.

"That's a good one!" Erin said, looking

at the cover. The book was called *Irish Fairy Legends*. "Maeve Rowe McCarron is very famous. She writes about Irish culture and history. I loved her books when I was younger."

"Until I read this book, I never knew there were so many kinds of fairy creatures in Irish folklore," Jessie said.

"We knew about leprechauns," Violet pointed out. "They're the ones who wear green and hide a pot of gold at the end of a rainbow."

"Mhm," Jessie said. "But we had never heard about the goblin that disguises itself as a chained black horse—the one called a pooka."

"And the creature called a merrow," Henry added. "It lives in the sea like a mermaid, but instead of a fish tail, it wears seal skins."

Grandfather noticed that both Benny and Violet were looking nervous. They weren't sure whether they wanted to meet creatures like these on their trip. "But remember," Grandfather said, "these creatures are part of myths. Myths are stories, but not everything in them is real."

"Just like ghosts," Henry said. "We know

from solving mysteries that when we think we see a ghost, there's always another explanation."

Just then, the waitress brought their food. All the children had ordered fish and chips, which came in wicker baskets lined with waxed paper. Grandfather and Erin had ordered mussels, and those came in bowls full of broth. They also had brown bread and fresh butter. The food smelled delicious.

"I don't know," Erin said, as she used a fork to pull a mussel from its black shell, "in Ireland, lots of people believe in banshees."

Jessie took a bite of fish and flipped a few pages in her book to the paragraph she was looking for. *"A banshee is a female spirit,"* she read aloud. *"Her cry can sound like a woman wailing or an owl moaning. She is often depicted wearing a gray hooded cloak. The presence of a banshee is known to be a bad omen."*

"What's a bad omen?" asked Benny. "It sounds...*bad*."

"I think it means bad luck," Henry said.

"Some of the old Irish families had their very own banshees," Erin said. "Like the family that once owned Duncarraig Castle.

Their banshee warned them when something bad was about to happen."

"Do you think *we* will see the banshee?" Benny asked.

Erin laughed. "Let's hope not!"

But Violet couldn't help noticing that Erin's fork was trembling when she took a bite. Talking about the banshee seemed to make her awfully uneasy.

GERTRUDE CHANDLER WARNER discovered when she was teaching that many readers who like an exciting story could find no books that were both easy and fun to read. She decided to try to meet this need, and her first book, *The Boxcar Children*, quickly proved she had succeeded.

Miss Warner drew on her own experiences to write the mystery. As a child she spent hours watching trains go by on the tracks opposite her family home. She often dreamed about what it would be like to set up housekeeping in a caboose or freight car—the situation the Alden children find themselves in.

While the mystery element is central to each of Miss Warner's books, she never thought of them as strictly juvenile mysteries. She liked to stress the Aldens' independence and resourcefulness and their solid New England devotion to using up and making do. The Aldens go about most of their adventures with as little adult supervision as possible—something else that delights young readers.

Miss Warner lived in Putnam, Connecticut, until her death in 1979. During her lifetime, she received hundreds of letters from girls and boys telling her how much they liked her books.